Cajun
Countin' 1-10
Author and Illustrator: Lilly Ahna

DEDICATION

This book is dedicated to the Spring Semester of 1998, Children's Literature class at Delgado Community College, City Park campus, in New Orleans, Louisiana. Under the tutelage of Ms. Julie Smith-Price

ACKNOWLEDGEMENT

To my dear friend LaTanya Sanders-Prograis; for supporting the silly presentation to our class. Also; thanks to my students, for the opportunity to share the fun and excitement of growing & learning on the Bayou.

Louisiana is a Southern State of the United States of America. It is located where the Mississippi River empties into the Gulf of Mexico. Louisiana is known as the original Bayou State because of its many bayous. Bayous are slow moving water inlets and outlets of lakes and/or rivers. Life in Louisiana is based on the original settlers known as "Cajuns." Ancestors of "Cajuns" were of Canadian and French descent.

The written dialect of this book is intended to introduce children to the linguistics of many Cajun families to this day.

*The World Book Encyclopedia; © 1983; vol. L–12, p. 482

One moon glow-in on a warm Summer night.
Glows brightly, on this muggy Cajun bayou tonight.

two squirrels a-playin with no fright in the night.

Near **Three** <u>creep-in gators,</u>
hop-in them squirrels don't up and run.

Four <u>hang-in</u> opossums
warn them squirrels at play,
that if they don't <u>a-scurry,</u> soon they'll become prey.

Five of <u>armadillas look-in</u> one just like the otha; meet...

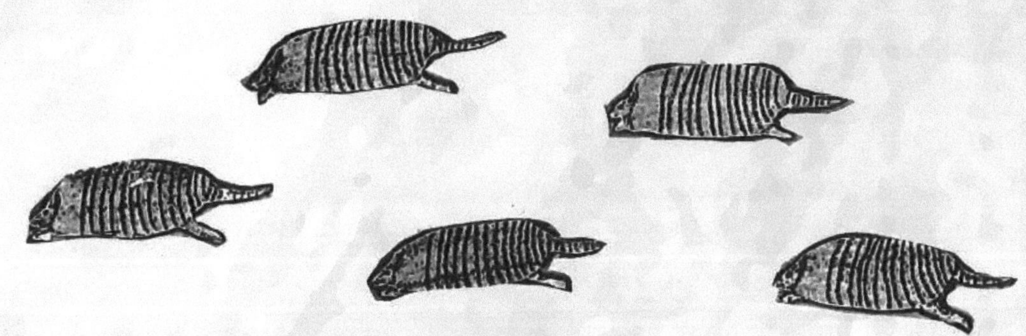

Six of <u>nutra-rats</u> and decide to play <u>togetha.</u>

Seven crawfish <u>crawl-in</u>
from their home down <u>in-a</u> mud;

Find **Eight** turtles <u>sleep-in</u>
with their heads all tucked in snug.

Nine dragonflies
Just <u>fly-in hav-in</u> fun, with...

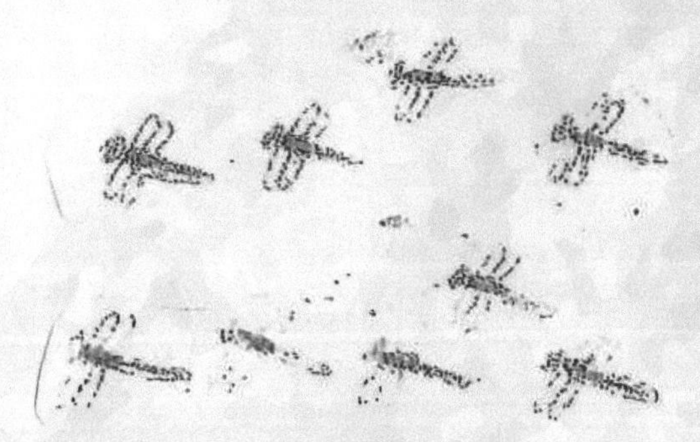

Ten Mosquitas swarmin and waitin
on the sun.
All these critters make a busy swam clan.

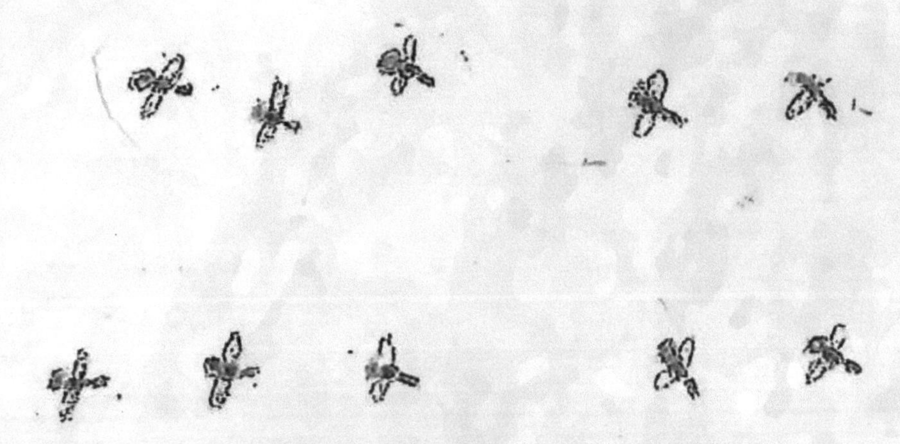

Beneath the One Moon, _a-glow-in_

on this muggy cajun bayou tonight.

Cajun Count-in Down on the Bayou

(song to the tune of Mari Gras Mambo)

Down on the bayou in Louisiana land.

The moon glows brightly on this busy swamp <u>clan.</u>

Out come two squirrels, and they begin to play-

While three <u>creep-in</u> gators quietly hide in lay.

Down on the bayou, bayou, bayou...

Down on the bayou, bayou, bayou...

Down on the ba-yoou-

in Louisiana land.

Now, four opossum <u>swing-in</u> warn the squirrels at play that if they

don't <u>a-scurry;</u> soon they'll become prey.

Down on the bayou, bayou, bayou...

Down on the bayou, bayou, bayou...

Down on the ba-yoou-

in Louisiana land.

Five of <u>armadillas look-in</u> one just like the <u>otha</u>...

Meet six of <u>nutra-rats</u> and soon begin to play...

Seven craw-fish <u>crawl-in</u> from their muddy home;

find eight sleep-in turtles, too tired to roam.

Down on the bayou, bayou, bayou...

Down on the bayou, bayou, bayou...

Down on the ba-yoou-

in Louisiana land.

Nine dragonflies, just <u>a-fly-in hav-in</u> fun...

With ten Mosquitas swarmin and a-waitin on the sun.

All of these critters make this busy swamp clan,

beneath the moon a-glow-in on this muggy cajun night.

Down on the bayou, bayou, bayou...

Down on the bayou, bayou, bayou...

Down on the ba-yoou-

in Louisiana land.

How many critters can you count?

Are there 10, or are there 55?

Numeral Count Groups
1
2
3
4
5

6
7
8
9
10

Number words group count

Five

Four

Three

Two

One

Cultural Translations of Words

Glow-in (Glowing): Brightness or warmth of colors.

Muggy: Having a lot of moisture in the air at ground level.

A-play-in (Playing): Engaging with others in a fun, cooperative manner.

Fright (Fear): To be scared.

Creep-in (Creeping): A slow, quiet crawl as if to sneak.

Gators (Alligators): Reptile animals found in the United States from North Carolina to the Rio Grande in Texas. Alligators usually live in freshwater, slow-moving rivers.

Hang-in (Hanging): Dangling (suspended) from above by the lower part of the object.

A-Scurry (Scurry): To move quickly.

Armadillas (Armadillos): Related to anteaters, they are the only mammal to wear a shell.

Look-in (Looking): Appearing the same or using one's eyes to observe.

Otha (Other): Someone who is not one's self.

Nutra-rats (Nutria rat): Large river rat (rodent) from South America.

Togetha (Together): To be with another.

Crawl-in (Crawling): Moving about using one's hands and feet in-a (Inside of):
Not able to be seen above or outside of.

Sleep-in (Sleeping): Not awake.

Fly-in (Flying): Suspending in air and moving above ground.

Hav-in (Having): To be experiencing an action.

Mosquitas (Mosquitos): A family of flies with a needle-like mouth used for biting
and sucking blood.

Swarm-in (Swarming): A group of insects fly together in the same direction.

www.ingramcontent.com/pod-product-compliance
Lightning Source LLC
Chambersburg PA
CBHW042029050726
47599CB00005B/849